Big Help!

To the young generation of cousins
who made me feel so special.
May each of you make your own
dreams come true.

Clarion Books
a Houghton Mifflin Company imprint
215 Park Avenue South, New York, NY 10003
Text and illustrations copyright © 1995 by Anna Grossnickle Hines

The illustrations for this book were executed in watercolor and colored pencil
on Fabriano Artistico paper.
The text was set in 14/19-point Americana.

Printed in Hong Kong

Library of Congress Cataloging-in-Publication Data

Hines, Anna Grossnickle.
Big help / by Anna Grossnickle Hines.
p. cm.
Summary: Sam's little sister pesters him with her offers to "help,"
but he finds a caring way to keep her from bothering him.
ISBN 0-395-68702-0
[1. Brothers and sisters—Fiction.] I. Title.
PZ7.H572Bg 1995
[E]—dc20   94-3632
                                                   CIP
                                                    AC

DNH 10 9 8 7 6 5 4 3 2 1

Big Help!

Anna Grossnickle Hines

Clarion Books/New York

Sam made a tunnel in the sand
for his cars.

"Me help!" said Lucy.

Sam put the twentieth block on his very tall tower.

"Me help!" said Lucy.

11

Sam dried the dishes for Daddy.
"Me help!" said Lucy.
"You're too little," said Sam.
"Me big! Me help!" Lucy screamed.
"Let her put away the plastic ones," said
Daddy. "She can't hurt herself on those."

Sam sighed. Lucy helped.

15

Sam got out his crayons to make a picture.
It was a big picture with boats and clouds.

"Me help!" said Lucy.

"No!" yelled Sam.
"That's Sam's picture, Lucy," Daddy said.
"Here, you can make your own."
"No," said Lucy. "Me help Sam."

"Come on, Lucy-Lu. Let's go piggy-back," said Daddy.

"No! No! No!" Lucy kicked and screamed.

"Wait a minute," said Sam, and disappeared.

"Good thinking, Sam," said Daddy.
"Me help," Lucy said.

22

"Okay," Sam agreed. "You pull. I'll ride."
"No! Me ride," said Lucy.

So Sam pulled.

He pulled and pulled . . .

27

and pulled.

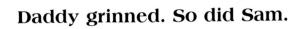
Daddy grinned. So did Sam.

29

Then he finished his picture with no help at all.